This book is dedicated to all of our family and friends.

Anthony@sanchostorybooks.com
Jennifer@sanchostorybooks.com

Library of Congress control number 2005908000

ISBN 13 digit 9780977324309
ISBN 10 digit 0-9773243-0-3

Second Printing Published in 2006 by Sancho Storybooks.
Printing and Binding by Midas Printing, China.

Sancho the Snowboarder

Written by Anthony Coccia
Illustrated by Jennifer McLaren

Jennifer McLaren

Anthony Coccia

It all began one Christmas morning in Vermont.

Sancho awoke and his first thought was,

I will run to the tree and see what Santa has brought!

As Sancho zoomed across the room,

He could see

A long narrow present under the tree!

What could it be?

Sancho ripped open his gift, he was swift!

Could it be? A snowboard for me?

On the couch

Was a snowboard suit,

A letter directly from Santa, and a pouch.

He raced for Santa's letter with lightning speed,
Then opened it up and began to read.

Dear Sancho,

This magic snowboard has one condition; I need your help on a secret mission!
In New York City on Christmas Eve, we were very busy and I had to leave.
All the elves and I were trying to reach Vermont on time, when we realized that,
By mistake, my two best elves got left behind.
Christmas Eve was very hurried and by now the missing elves must be very worried.
I need you to find them, if you could, and help them get home if you would.
On the couch is a magic suit, it can handle any storm and will keep you warm!
Also one pouch of magic powder,
Why?
To make your snowboard fly!
Just sprinkle it on and you'll be gone!
The magic powder is for you, but give some to the elves too. They will know what to do.
You'll have to be fast and very witty to find the elves in New York City!

Good Luck,
Santa Claus

With no time to sit,
Sancho tried on his snowboard suit,
It was a perfect fit!
He grabbed his magic powder,
Not spilling any on the floor,
He grabbed his snowboard and ran out the door!

The magic snowboard was so easy to ride.

It was super fast with perfect glide.

Sancho laughed, "It's super slick,"

As he had fun landing every trick!

The bottom of the hill had no flow,

But the magic powder would make the snowboard go!

Santa said, just sprinkle it on,

And you'll be gone!

Why?

To make your snowboard fly!

Flying over towns,
The wind and the air, the only sounds.
Riding higher than any kite,
Riding fast at the speed of light!
Looking down,
Sancho saw people in every town.
Sooo far down, the moving blots,
They looked just like little spots.

The lights were bright and the sky was red.

New York City was just ahead!

Sancho was feeling really small,

When he saw all the buildings so very tall!

Sancho looked for a landing mark,
And in the middle of the city, he saw a park.
He saw some water with a swan.
And landed beside it on the great big lawn!

Sancho looked with all his might.

Then he asked the first man in sight,

"Have you seen Santa's elves?"

He said that he had and last he knew,

They were on their way to the City Zoo!

Some more magic powder and off he flew,
Then straight back down to the City Zoo.

Sancho landed on the monkey path,

Beside a meadow with a big giraffe.

On the ground he made haste.

He started looking with no time to waste!

Running past a big brown bear,
Sancho saw the zookeeper there.

"Excuse me, sir, I'm looking for two elves," he said.

"They are wearing green and red."

"I have seen them," the zookeeper said.

"I have seen them in their green and red.

They're off to Liberty Island you see.

They're off to see the Statue of Liberty!"

Now that Sancho had left the zoo,

He was flying fast toward the Statue.

He sprinkled some more magic powder on,

And in a second he was gone!

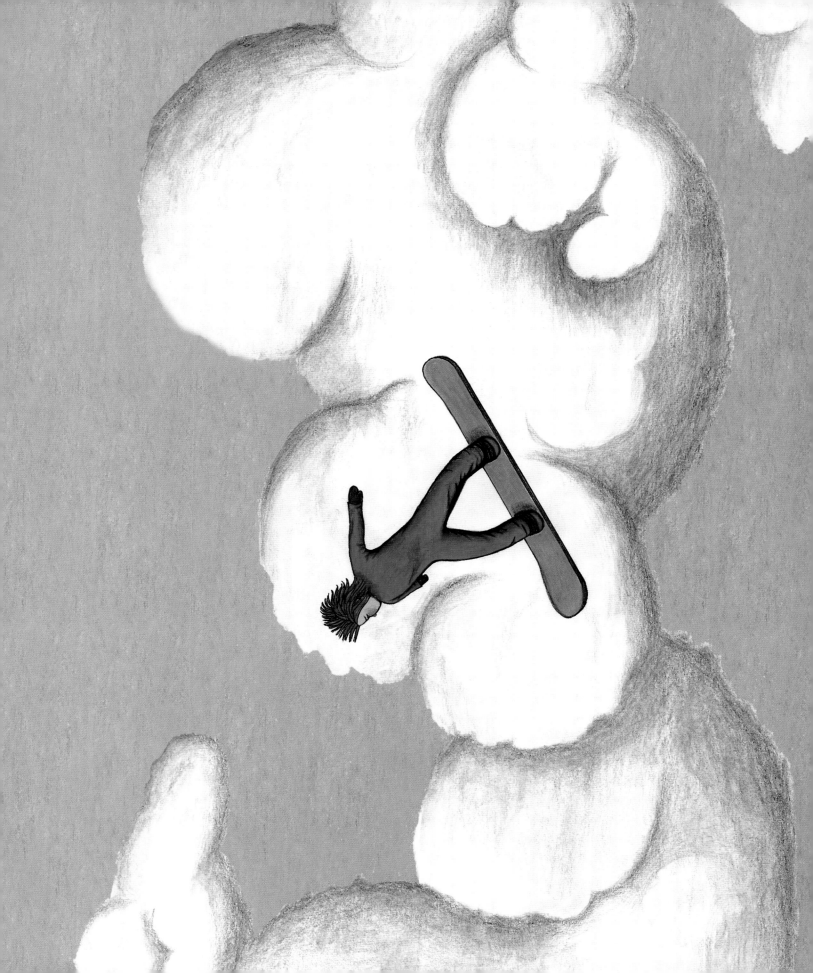

The Hudson River was just below,
So Sancho turned his board down low.
He surfed the waves in the sun,
Passing boats and having fun!

Down the river as he sped,
The Statue of Liberty was just ahead.
The boats and people all looked so small,
The Statue is 305 feet tall!

He rode up on the shore.
And ran fast toward the Statue floor.
Sancho looked hard with all his might,
But the elves were nowhere in sight!

Sancho saw a woman tour guide.

And made his way up to her side.

"I'm looking for two elves," he said.

"They are small and wearing green and red."

"They were here," the tour guide said.

"I saw them in their green and red.

The Empire State Building, they wanted to see.

The Empire State Building is where they'll be."

Before Sancho flew back through the West Side,

He kindly asked the tour guide,

"Do you know how this Statue got here, by chance?"

She said, "Yes I do. It was a gift from France!"

Back across the river, as fast as he could go!

The wind on his tail, it was an easy flow.

He could see the Empire State building,

Standing tall in the sky.

So Sancho turned his board up high.

The Empire State Building is very tall.
In fact, it's one of the tallest of them all!
Sancho looked just like a little speck,
Before he landed on the lookout deck.

All the people were very wowed.

As Sancho landed in the crowd.

Looking hard for a clue,

Sancho ran up to a man in blue.

"I'd like to ask you if I may?

Have you seen two elves today?"

"Yes, I have," he quickly said.

"They are here and wearing green and red.

In the corner last I knew,

Taking in the city view!"

He saw their pointy ears and funny shoes

And ran up to them with the news,

"My name is Sancho and I've come to say

That Santa has sent me to find you today.

Here's some magic powder for both of you.

Santa said you would know what to do!"

They took some magic powder and sprinkled it on,
Then snapped their fingers and they were gone!
And for a second, where they stood,
It sparkled and glittered, just like magic should.

Now that Sancho's mission was done,

It was time for his long ride home in the setting sun.

Some more magic powder,

Why?

To make your snowboard fly!

Just sprinkle it on

And you'll be gone!

Up ahead was the sky police,

An entire flock of Canadian geese!

They all honked with grace and style,

As Sancho waved and gave a smile.

Back toward Vermont, as he sped,
He could see the snow covered mountains just ahead.
After New York, and full of pride,
He could hardly wait to land and ride!

Flying high has many thrills,

But not as much fun as riding down the hills!

Back toward home, through all the sticks,

He had fun landing all his tricks!

Back in his house,

Sancho put his snowboard on the floor

And hung his suit up by the door.

Across the room, he was able

To see another letter on the table.

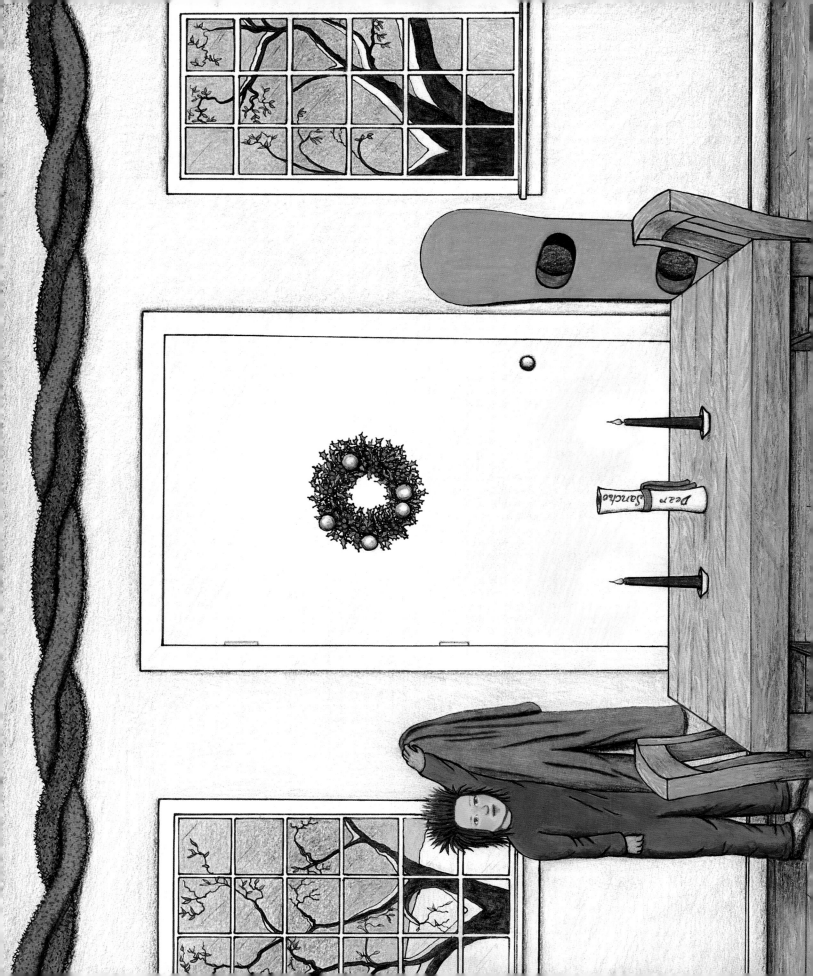

He opened the letter, hoping to read,
That Santa was happy
For his very good deed.

Dear Sancho,

The elves are back here at the North Pole.

Thanks for sticking to your goal.

I understand you had quite an adventure.

I knew you could do it, that I was sure!

We never know what will happen around this place,

So keep the magic snowboard just in case!

Thanks again Sancho

Santa Claus

Sancho lay asleep in his bed,

With dreams of adventure in his head.

Dreams of a journey, of where he'll go.

Dreams of riding his snowboard tomorrow!